I AM GOD, I AM JESUS, I AM ALLAH;

THE TRUTH WILL SET YOU FREE

Volume II

ALLAH TAKES UP FLESH

JEFF OLSON

Satan appeared and he looked at Paul who was one and half and threw him out the open window. Satan was going to end it and drawn his sword. Allah (Jeff) just looked at Satan and angels appeared. They caught Paul and rested him on the ground below. They then hauled Satan away to go in front of God. A lady saw Paul fall out the window and they got Bev and seen Paul was fine. Bev took Paul to the hospital and they said he was fine.

Jeff and his family then lived on a farm house about 7 miles from Madelia Minnesota after that. Jeff was curious in this new world and was constantly getting into trouble exploring the things in this new world he was discovering himself in. Jeff was about three and one half years old where something terrible was about to happen. Jeff his brother Paul and baby Mark were with Mom and Dad Christmas shopping. Mom had purchased this sparkly glass that Jeff wanted a better look at, so he crawled on top of the table using a chair. Jeff was holding the sparkly glass used to hold wine in his hands. He was sitting on the table looking at this glass it was beautiful. Suddenly with everyone's back turned away from Jeff on the table unpacking the other gifts. Satan appears and yells you little shit and pushes Jeff off the table. Jeff screams as he hits the floor still holding the glass. The glass cuts Jeff's hand and pointer finger. He is bleeding profusely out his hand. His Mother grabs a cloth diaper and wraps the hand as they all head to the Madelia clinic to get stitches before Jeff bleeds out. Jeff blacks out and Doctor James Eiseit stitched Jeff's hand together. Jeff had to go to Saint Mary's hospital in Mankato for surgery they cut up past Jeff's wrist looking for glass. There was nothing the doctors could do Jeff lost the ability to grip with his pointer finger and would be that way for the rest of his human life. Jeff went home after surgery and the stitches itched so bad Jeff felt like cutting them out.

CHAPTER 2

Jeff was told to go outside his stitches were out and he felt ok again. He heard a voice Allah the voice said. Allah looked around and didn't see anyone he heard another voice say Father it is me Noel and God. Jeff wondered what was going on as he suddenly remembered both of them. Allah are you ok asked God. Allah said yes God. Father do you remember why you're here asked Noel. Allah said I think so but help me remember. Suddenly all the memories came back to Allah. Allah was four and suddenly became more focused on God's plan but was watchful for Satan. We spent allot of nights at grandpa and grandma Olson's as Dad finished boiler man's school. God said Allah I want you to unravel all of Satan's changes he made to all the religious books you helped write, Satan has changed them, I want you to join all the books together by retelling the stories, Noel, Oceanna, the angels and I will tell you what to write and how to tell the stories. Allah Satan will be fighting you the whole time but you will prevail.

God was playing Satan in what would be known here on Earth as a game of pool at billiards. God was leading by one and God needed to put the eight ball into the hole. Satan had told a snake to hide in the hole and force the eight ball back on the table. God and Allah were talking and were not watching Satan as he placed the snake in the hole. Satan closed the window and looked both to the left and right and did not see any eagles. God looked at Satan as he turned around from looking out the window. Satan had never beat God in any game especially pool. Satan had a huge smile on his face. God looked at Satan and said "Satan I win if I can get around your ball and put the eight ball in that corner pocket. Just as God made his shot. Satan jumped up I win, I Win. Then a mongoose landed on the table swooped over to the corner pocket, grabbed the snake and headed out the door. The eight ball went right in the corner pocket. Satan hit the floor, God said "Are you alright Satan?" Satan said yes, you win again God. They don't call the game pool in heaven it is called snake in the corner pocket.

CHAPTER 3

Jeff's brothers Chad and Eric were born and then the family moved to Madelia and lived in a white brick house on Center Street. The family seemed to thrive Mother got a job at Golden Pantry and Father continued to work at Tony Downs in Madelia as a boiler man. Dad finally got his big break and started working at Kraft in New Ulm Minnesota. Jeff did many paper routes to include the Star and Tribune, Free Press, the Shoppers Guide, And the Sunday paper Star and Tribune. In the summer Jeff along with his brothers detached the tassel on corn to make money with their Mother and Grandmother Lorraine Fredrickson. Jeff (Allah) did not see Satan for a while in his life. We had a terrible snow storm and so we all piled into Dad's four wheel drive Chevy pick-up truck and headed to LaSalle Minnesota to be there for Christmas Eve celebration. The truck was blue with a white stripe down the middle 1976 Chevy Truck. No one else could make it out to Grandma Lorraine and Grandpa Marlow's house so we postponed the celebration for a couple days but it was always on Christmas Eve otherwise.

I went to the bowling alley to play arcade games with my friend Scott Visher and got into a fight with another kid from school and in the middle of the fight I grabbed my wrist of my other hand and all the kids yelled "the Claw" from Barron von Ratshski an all-star wrestler from television. The fight ended with me getting taken home in a police car.

In the summer Jeff fished and camped down at the Watonwan River with his friend Scott Visher. When I was around 14, I was sleeping on the couch of our home in Madelia, Minnesota. Satan pulled me out of my body and I told him to leave me alone this was not a dream when I wake up I was standing straight up and heard Satan laughing. My other friend was Jim Yates who I went to the same class as mine Jim and I would become best friends. I went out for football and wrestling in school. When I was in my last three years of High School I met a great friend in Paul Jeramo. We took a Spanish class Paul Jeramo, Jim Yates, and myself (Jeff) and so I called Paul, Pablo and he called me Juilio. Satan made his appearance once again my friend Scott Visher killed himself and he was laughing when my friend's brother Ryan Visher called with the news. Scott had shop lifted a cassette tape from Shopko in Mankato. His mother told him his life was over and he was going to go to a boy's home. Scott went upstairs in his house loaded the gun and killed himself. I was devastated and have never fully recovered from this trajedy in my life. Pablo and myself, (Jeff) went to concerts together Judas Priest, ACDC, Stripper, And Van Hallen. I got a minor consumption of alcohol with my friend Jim Yates and Dad decided I needed a job to take up my time after school and weekends and got a job at Tony Downs. My Mother and Father got divorced and I Jeff stayed with my Dad.

CHAPTER 4

Jeff graduate's high school and joins the United States Marines with his best friend Jim Yates. God told Jeff to join the Marines and his best friend Jim Yates followed him into the service. Boot camp was fun for both Jeff and Jim and Jim was the best marksman in his platoon and graduated with those honors. Jeff continued to have those dreams about his son (Noel) being killed on the cross and the people drowning in Noah's time. Jeff got a job at Taco Bell off base at Fall Brook California as he was stationed at Camp Pendleton California. This is where he met his second girl-friend, Dolly Clark his first Love was Debbie Johnson who he dated a couple times but it never developed as Jeff had hoped. Jeff was in love he worked as a small arms repairman in the day and at night he spent working and dating Dolly. He would spend all night at Dolly's sisters house Melinda and then back to work at the Marines. Life had finally taken a turn for the good he thought. Then Dolly went back to Texas and reunited with an old boyfriend and letters were sent but nothing developed after Dolly had a baby boy and left that man on bad terms. Jeff felt slighted and decided to move on. He found and married Paula Zamzow who wrote Jeff while he served aboard the USS. Saratoga Air Craft Carrier while serving as a Marine in a "Special Forces Unit," while in the Gulf War. Jeff was named Marine of the Year in this Special Forces Unit aboard the USS. Saratoga. Jeff married his then wife Paula

Zamzow at the "Little White Chapel," in Los Vegas Nevada. Allah (Jeff) was told by God and agreed to by Oceanna that Jeff would marry and have a wife who would have his son who would be the King of Israel. This would be the promise fulfilled by God to give them a king with bloodline to continue for all time. Jeff got Orders to Twenty-Nine Palms California where he brought his then wife Paula and her daughter Mallory to live with him in Twenty-Nine Palms military base housing. Things went well at first and then the marriage started to break down. Paula's Mother Judy wanted the baby born in Wisconsin where she lived. Jeff insisted the child be born at the base hospital to save money and so Jeff could be there when the baby was born so Satan could not kill the baby. Jeff could not tell the reasons why but only that it was important. The next problem occurred with naming the child. The Zamzow family wanted it to be Jacob, Jeff insisted that it be Jake short for Jacob to throw Satan off of the child for the time being until the child was older again to keep Satan away from the child. Then the fighting began between Paula and Jeff. Paula's Mother Judy called on Thanksgiving Day crying telling her daughter that no one was there to spend Thanksgiving with. This started a fight between Jeff and Paula that killed the marriage. Jeff was upstairs watching the Viking game on the television set. Mallory was watching a movie on the big television down stairs. Paula got the phone call from her Mother while the turkey was roasting in the oven. Paula pulled a butcher knife out of the drawer in the kitchen. Paula headed up stairs to the bedroom where Jeff was. She angrily told Jeff about her conversation with her Mother Judy. Jeff said it will be alright just relax and enjoy your time here we do not have money for you to go to Wisconsin to be with your Mom Paula. Paula held the knife up and said you are going to do what I say or else. I suddenly felt Oceanna's presents and then she was inside of me. I took the knife out of Paula's hand and spanked Paula over my knee with my hand very hard. Paula was upset and said she was sorry, I said I was sorry to but once Paula's family heard what I did minus what Paula did with the knife she never mentioned that even in court at the divorce proceedings. Paula said, "She was the victim here and she was going to make me pay."

CHAPTER 5

Jeff has papers served on Paula for divorce since she took the children from their home on base housing in Twenty-Nine Palms California while Jeff was attending class to get his Bachelor's degree in Criminal Justice. Jeff goes to court in San Bernadino County in Joshue Tree California. Jeff is told that Minnesota is going to assume jurisdiction over the proceedings in Hennipen County where the Mother and children now reside. If Jeff wants to see his children he must come to Minnesota to see them. Jeff goes to Minnesota to visit the children through his Attorney Alan Albrecht. The visitation never takes place until three hours before Jeff leaves to go back to the base in Twenty-Nine Palms California over several days of arguing between attorneys, Jeff gets to see his son Jake for an hour with his grandparents. Jeff heads back to base and continues his studies for his degree and is told to mail all of Paula's belongings and the children's at his expense. Jeff gets out of the Marines after several more times being denied visitation with his son. Jeff finished his degree and kept a 3.5 grade point average throughout his studies. Jeff finished his 4 year degree in 2.5 years. Allah got an Honorable discharge and went back to Minnesota to finish Gods plan. Jeff just wanted to see his son as a normal Father without interference, but that never ever occurred.

CHAPTER 6

Jeff settled back in first living with his Mom and step Father Daryl Olson. Jeff lived there about a week and a half and found it more comfortable to live with his Father and Step Mother Ruth and her four children. Jeff lived there about 2 months and then bought a modest house near Mankato Minnesota. Jeff started working at Precision Press running a printing press for the manufacture of personalized post it notes. He also worked at Mankato Oil and Tire CO., the United States Post Office, and Brown Printing all at the same time. Jeff had very little sleep between jobs and lived on Mountain Dew, and power naps, he did this for 5 years until finally settling in at the post office. Jeff also dealt with his child custody case and trying to get unsupervised visitation. Allah's will to see his son and finish God's plan came before any pain he was feeling about work or the courts. Jeff sued his Ex-wife, her attorney and many judges all the way to the United States Supreme Court twice. Allah's case was that Minnesota lacked jurisdiction, and the judges erred in the proceedings denying him visitation rights to his son. The United States Supreme Court chose not to hear the case. Jeff is barred from filing a federal case in federal court. The judges barred Gods Servant, God will have something to say about that when the time comes, when these judges are judged themselves.

CHAPTER 7

Allah remembers his teachings to the Hindu "The Rig Veda" or teachings of the separation of Heaven and Earth. Heaven and Earth are separated by many things. To get this understanding to the people these myths were created by Allah to explain it to the teachers for the people. The Gods in the Hindu Religion are actually angels who can take on different body structures. Angels can also be shape shifters and you need to account for that in this religion. God's word is always worship him and him only over time man has become attracted to the angels and threw Satan the evil person we must be careful to worship only God not God's Angels. Good Karma and bad karma hold true today and always, you do not want bad karma. Allah teaches God's laws to the people however he can, in this religion it is threw stories about angels and God. The language of the people sometimes does not allow for words and precise writings but stories instead. This is an old religion and as with all of God's teachings it is meant to satisfy for now but to be mindful and watchful as God's teachings continue to this day threw Allah and his family. Allah loved being with the Hindu people and teaching them Gods laws and how to live and treat others with respect and dignity.

CHAPTER 8

Allah remembers his teachings to his servant Buddha, Allah loved Buddha he would laugh and laugh and Allah just could not get enough of his humor in everything he did. Buddha was a large man but a wise and calm spirited person. Allah misses his time with Buddha and the many years he spent teaching Buddha about life, God, heaven and people. I am going to tell you a funny story about Allah and Buddha. So one day I was speaking to Buddha and he had photographic memory. He remembered everything like Paul the apostle or Nostradamus. So Buddha goes stop right there Allah and I stopped what is it Buddha, he said we have to go. I did not since any danger but off we went, what is it Buddha I said, in a minute Allah. We went about seven miles over a couple hills and we came to this farm. Buddha stop now tell me what it is, we are walking so far for. Buddha turned around can't you smell the lovely pies baking in this farmers brick oven. Buddha I said you are hungry again, Allah I am always hungry for pies said Buddha. Buddha taught his followers all of what Allah had taught him and was a great leader for spiritual growth and discipline and learning for his followers which all can learn from. I miss Buddha and cannot wait to see him at the table of God where his seat is reserved as a part of my family of God.

CHAPTER 9

The Koran has two prophets, I Allah only have one Prophet and that is Muhammad. The first Six SURA Muhammad did not write and they did not come from Allah. If you look closely SURA 2 and 7 have similar passages this is the work of Satan. All who believe in Allah are to remove the first 6 SURA they are the work of Satan. You will also find references to the Holy Spirit who replaced Allah in the Bible. Allah would have never allowed this nor would Muhammad of written that abomination in the Koran. Satan has been very busy and its evidence is clear as day, I am an angel of peace and a man of peace, I only go to war as a last resort. The first 6 SURA do not match what is in heaven with God in Paradise. Muhammad agrees he did not right that hateful writing he said Allah you know I would not write that. A false prophet has written those words for Satan to mislead our followers. Allah's book of the Koran actually starts at SURA 7, which was SURA 1 before Allah took Muhammad to heaven. The Koran was rewritten and added on from the front by a prophet of Satan. Satan's prophet is clever and added Holy Spirit to a few more spots in the Koran but this should be taken out when they are meant to replace Allah. As is said in the Bible 666 is the first 6 SURA from Satan's Prophet, 777 starting from SURA 7 which was SURA 1 before I took Muhammad to heaven is Allah's number to the end of the book of the Koran.

CHAPTER 10

Jeff Olson had none of his requests to see his son Jake Tyler unsupervised in the Hennepin County Family Courts met. Jeff Olson made over 50 requests to see his son unsupervised until his son turned 18 then after he graduated Jeff and Jake Tyler have had a great relationship. Hennepin County never gave a reason why Jeff could not see his son unsupervised and Jeff can only assume they work for Satan. Satan would badger Allah before each hearing saying "Allah why are you wasting your time they work for me, they will never let you see your son unsupervised and then Satan would laugh."

Jeff never quit trying and God told Allah you will have a relationship with your son Allah press on the Hennepin County Judges, the guardian, and her attorney cannot change the eventual outcome and neither can your ex-wife. I will never forget when the bailiff said all rise for these judges to me it felt like a Nazi salute as Satan laughed and cheered on these judges it just made me sick. Jeff sued his ex-wife, her attorney Gerald O. Williams, and many Judges and others all the way to the United Supreme Court twice as was mentioned.

CHAPTER 11

Jeff worked at the United States Post Office and God said I want you to start visiting places in the world to jog your memory and refresh work you did in the past and memories about your son Noel (Jesus) as Israel was my first place to visit. 01/22/2020 it was about 0900 pm I had been typing on my computer and was typing about my first book how it was the book Satan coveted and the book Apostle John ate up and instead gave Satan the book of Revelations. Satan started swearing and smashing things in the house until he left to talk to God. If you look closely in the Bible you will find this written, God has the same name as I it is Allah. Exodus 23:20 For God said I send an Angel and my name is in him, this name is Allah. God and I share the same name which can be confusing when you read the Bible. The veil has dropped Muslims, Christians, and Jews all pray to the same God, along with the Hindu and Buddhists. There is only one God and his name is Allah the same as mine but I am not God, I am God's servant. You have always prayed to the same God, you just did not know his name until now.

CHAPTER 12

God holds court one day in the future. Noel (Jesus) finishes for the prosecution. Jesus says Grandfather, father says Allah has been stripped completely from the Bible. Satan looks at Jesus and says grandfather? Jesus says yes grandfather! Satan looks at God, "Allah is your son?" God looks at Satan as anger begins to build upon God's face. "Satan you took my name out of the Bible," said God? Satan looks at God and says "Your name is Allah?" God says yes Satan it is I didn't tell you everything. God says "Satan I am going to kill you for doing that, you know that don't you?" Satan says "It wasn't me who did it, it was those two Popes." The two Popes say "Satan told us to do it." Satan looked at Jesus and "Jesus said Satan you better run." Satan ran out of the palace as fast as he could. God raised his hand in a swing motion and Satan was dead at 1000 am on 01/24/2020. Everyone in heaven cheered and tears of joy fell upon all the people.

CHAPTER 13

Allah remembers when he first met Oceanna, it was in Angel school. Allah sat behind Oceanna, he would extend his head forward to smell Oceanna's hair it was so pleasant to Allah's nose he would daydream they were together on a mountain side running through flowers in the valley below. Allah dreamed about how sweet Oceanna's lips would taste against his with a kiss. Allah was day dreaming one day and the teacher was looking for the answer to his question about God's laws. The teacher said Allah do you know the answer to my question. Allah didn't answer he was day dreaming about Oceanna. The teacher said very loudly Allah stand up and tell the class the answer. Satan saw the whole thing and said "Allah tell the class the answer as he laughed. Allah stood up and asked the teacher what the question was again. The teacher said go wait in the Chief Angels Office. Allah left as Satan tripped him and he fell right on Oceanna. Allah said I am so sorry Oceanna. Oceanna smiled and said it is ok as she kissed Allah on the cheek. The teacher seen it and sent Oceanna to the Chief Angels office with Allah. Oceanna grabbed Allah's hand and said let's go to the office then. That is how it all began for Allah and Oceanna.

CHAPTER 14

God opens training for Angel Military School this was a new school and only the best angels were selected. God did the selecting himself. The first angel picked was Satan. God wanted the angels trained in sword use to defend heaven should it ever come under attack. Satan was the first angel selected and Satan never let any angel forget it. Satan was an excellent sword fighter but so was Allah. God had competitions between sword fighters every couple weeks and almost always it came down to Satan and Allah as the victors. Satan carried a smaller sword than Allah which meant he was quicker but could not with stand punishing blows with the sword as heavy as Allah's for long in a competition. Allah would outlast Satan he knew if he could get past the first minute of sword combat. Satan knew he had to make a superior move with his sword very quickly if he was going to beat Allah. Allah and Satan would almost always partner up and they were still friends at this point. Come on Allah give me your best shot Satan would yell and Allah would swing his sword as it crashed and vibrated down threw Satan's hands. You do not stand a chance today Satan as the swords crashed together. The Angel sword master would challenge Allah swing harder. Allah swung and smashed the sword Satan had into two pieces, Satan stood in fear of sword fighting Allah anymore and wanted a new partner. Allah's skills as a sword fighter finally passed Satan's and Allah won every competition after that.

CHAPTER 15

Satan hide behind some bushes he could see Oceanna and Allah down by the stream they were kissing and talking about their soon to be baby Oceanna was carrying in her belly. Oceanna smiled at Allah "What are we going to tell God Allah," said Oceanna. Allah said "I think God already knows Oceanna," he knows everything let us tell him we want to be married. Satan beat Allah and Oceanna to God and told God the whole thing. Oceanna and Allah showed up and said leave us Satan. Allah Oceanna do you have something you want to tell me? Yes said Allah and Oceanna God we want to be married. God said are you in love and want to spend all eternity together as husband and bride? Yes they both said and God smiled and married them and said Oceanna are you expecting a child. Oceanna started to cry and said yes God but I love Allah. God said "Its ok feeling Oceanna's belly I understand, it is going to be a man child, what name are-you going to name him?" Oceanna said I am going to name him Noel.

CHAPTER 16

Oceanna and Allah were given a cottage close to God's palace so God could watch his grandson Noel grow up. Noel was very smart and loved being with his father and grand-father. God would take Noel on many fishing trips where Noel learned how to spot fish and catch them. It was not a coincidence that Noel picked fisherman to be his Apostles, Noel loved fishing. In heaven Allah had a vision, he saw the two Popes Innocent taking his name out of the Bible along with God's and Oceanna's and changing the stories about Noel (Jesus). Satan if we do this will we still get into heaven the Popes asked Satan. Of course you will said Satan and you will be my two dragons in the book of Revelations. What will happen to us when we get to heaven asked the Popes? I want you both too start making the people worship you and make them kiss your ring. But what about heaven the popes said only God is worshiped in heaven? Satan said do not worry God is creating the universe only you have to worry is Allah, he is your enemy. The Popes did as Satan had asked them and took Allah's name and not knowing it Gods name out of the Bible. Satan smiled and laughed and said destroy the cup of Jesus Christ after you have drank the blood and tell the people they will become vampires if they drink blood and will go to hell. The popes looked at each other and said to Satan "What is Hell?" Satan smiled and said "Tell the people that is the place where I will be to torcher them for all time." The two Popes looked at each other and smiled and said I like that Satan.

CHAPTER 17

Allah asks God about his vision. God says evil against good surrounds everything we do Allah you will prevail in the end but there is much pain along the way if you want it all Allah. Allah says to God "Why does it half to cost me everything." This is the price to understand why you will know all I have given you comes responsibility. To truly love the humans costs everything you have that is the price. Allah knows what that means as he wipes tears from his eyes, I do love them God, than pay the price and God walked away. Allah says to God will I get it all back, God says yes but you still have to endure the pain, it will always be with you like a bad dream. Allah wipes away more tears, my son and my bride? God says yes and heaven, you must give it all up. Allah wipes away tears and says Father then I know what I have to do. Allah was crying and Oceanna and Noel said "Father what is wrong?" Allah wiped away his tears and said to both Oceanna and Noel "You know I love you both more than anything but I am being tested as you both will be also for the good of God's plan." Then Allah let it go like it was a dream.

CHAPTER 18

God and Jesus (Noel) told Allah it is time, we want you to travel the world. Allah asked God why? God said "I want to jog your memory and people will be attracted to you and they will not know why. Allah started his travels by going to Israel first. Allah had visited Israel or at least visited Haifa when he was in Israel when he was in the Marines. There was a terrible ferry boat accident where Satan tried to kill Allah once more. Allah went to church in Haifa and then met some other Marines outside a lounge in Haifia and

But Noel warned his father Allah that Satan was going to kill him and Jesus told Allah to stay on the U.S.S. Saratoga. Allah stayed on the ship as Jesus told him to do. Allah arrived in Israel as a tourist and got to know many of the other tourists. The tour was led by a Jewish man who Allah found very impressive. Most all the tourists were elderly and retired. They were not impressed with Allah as most of the people on the tour were Catholic. Allah did not hold that against them and tried to be positive and social. But as the tour continued it became apparent to Allah that some had a hidden agenda. On the tour one spot was visited where the tour guide pointed out caves in the desert and a Catholic Chicago man walked up to Allah and told him "Why don't you go up in that cave and die." Allah said nothing and tried to ignore the gentleman and focus on the tour. Then throughout the tour comments were made about Allah and again Allah tried to ignore them. At about the end of the tour Allah (Jeff) went with an older gentleman and his grandson to a Catholic Church that was run by a Priest and about three Nuns. Allah participated in Holy Communion and this seemed to win over these people who obviously had something against him. You see Jeff had taken out a web site where he had told the truth about Allah being Jesus Father and one of them confessed that they had thought I was Satan until I took up communion. I asked him why he thought I was Satan and the answer was the web-site and that Satan could never partake in Holy Communion. I did not know what plan they had for me but I was very sick which started on the plane ride home to Minnesota and lasted about a month. I traced the disease back to some water I may have drank that was not purified.

CHAPTER 19

My next trip was to Australia. Again I detected that Rome played an interest in my travels. I met an incredible friend from Canada on this trip, an older gentleman who told me he did not believe in religious churches but believed in God. He was a farmer and very much attracted to me because again I think he read the web site I posted. There again were Catholics but this time they kept a safe distance because of my friend. I think Rome had decided I was marking people but Rome does not understand that the mark is Gods and Satan's word. It is not a touch of the hand, tattoo or other identification. Satan changed the Bible this then is his mark. Satan did not get to mark my book but he coveted it and wanted it more than anything. Satan got the book of Revelations and John ate up "I am God, I am Jesus, I am Allah; the truth will set you free." Satan wants to know what is going on and does not know the book of Revelations because some of it is in code. The many governments took an interest in me, a person I believe to be Chinese was taking photos of me on a boat while I was on the tour trying to look conspicuous. I then knew about the measures taken to watch me. I do not have an army just God, Noel, Oceanna and the many angels charged to watch over me. But I must be a threat to them because all the angels told me they could sense the hate for me.

CHAPTER 20

My next visit was too China, this trip was curious to me as I went to China where I was at my most heavy weight. All the people of China thought I looked like Buddha and wanted their picture with me. This is also where the angels were most worried about me. We were on the tour bus and driving down the highway at night and someone was knocking on the outside of my window on the bus laughing. I knew who it was and tried to ignore him. Satan the trickster is no doubt behind the Coronavirus but God may have sent him. Most all of these virus's Satan and I worked on when I was back in heaven a long time ago. There are many of them, and my memory is good but I do not remember all of them. They are all bad diseases designed to transfer from animal to human. The worst ones are rat to human. Then Allah remembered Oceanna, they were under a tree in heaven and Oceanna said to Allah what do you think will happen after I have our baby. Allah smiled and kissed Oceanna and said we will live near God and I will love you forever Oceanna. Oceanna smiled and said I want to name him Noel. Allah said that is a beautiful name and I know he will love his name because it came from you Oceanna. Oceanna kissed Allah and they picked a piece of fruit above them and laughed as they each ate a piece. Allah sat under the tree and held Oceanna in his arms as he looked at the horizon.

CHAPTER 21

Allah meets with the Angel Gabriel at a secret location. Allah tells Gabriel that he is going to need him to get messages to God, that Satan or his demon friends no nothing about. Gabriel agrees and Allah says you're the angel I am going to use to get Gods word out if I need to meet with God in secret myself. Gabriel says I understand Allah. Gabriel then tells Allah just so you know I have the same agreement with Satan. Allah looks at Gabriel and says as long as you keep my secrets and do the work I need you to do your friendship with Satan I have no problem with. Gabriel leaves and then he talks to his son Noel. Noel you understand what is at stake here? Noel says yes father I think we can trust Gabriel. Allah says yes he is my best friend. Gabriel met God and said I have a message from Satan and one from Allah and one from Noel. God said good follow me I want to finish creating this star first. Gabriel said those are the messages and Allah is having trouble right now with reality, he just killed a turkey that he thought was Satan. God said I know but Allah will be alright he will get stronger with each day and then Satan better watch out. Do you think he will kill Satan asked Gabriel to God. God said that is not up to me to say who will kill Satan. Is good stronger than evil asked Gabriel? God said the path to do good, is longer than the path to do evil so yes it is. To do evil is short lived and then you pay for it these are my laws.

CHAPTER 22

Allah's next trip was to South Africa this was the most exhausting trip for Jeff. Again Catholic's were sent to watch Allah and Rome was kept in contact about what they thought were Satan's "Mark." Allah arrived in South Africa but his suitcase did not arrive with him. Allah had to wait 2 days to get his suitcase, when it arrived Allah could tell it was searched for anything to link him to the Muslim community. Then the tour started and the guide was perplexing in that he did not seem like a guide but an agent of the CIA. The tour guide had no paperwork to give to the people on the tour which is standard protocol for a guide to tell the people on the tour what would happen the next day. The other tourists commented on what was happening, and Allah knew something was up when the bus caught on fire and the bags had to be left behind and the tour group was loaded in a new bus to go to the safari houses. Allah knew his suitcase was searched again and the guide had a distaste for Jeff after the suitcases were brought to the houses that lasted for the remainder of the tour. Allah finally came to the conclusion that they thought Allah was going to join ISSIS while on the tour and when that did not happen it made the guide in disguise angry with Jeff. Jeff found this distasteful behavior amusing and was kind to the guide and blew it off as simply Satan causing trouble. While on the Safari Allah seen the elephants and he remembered bringing them from the planet the water came from to bring this planet out of the Ice Ages. The dirt or clay that had to be brought that the Elephants loved. An elephant bull came out of the trees and stared for a minute at Allah and then went down to the lake with the others. The guide said bull elephants are unpredictable were you scared Jeff? I just smiled and said nothing.

CHAPTER 23

Then Allah thought about Michel- De-Nostradamus and his time with him. Nostradamus said to Allah, "Thankyou Allah for all this knowledge but Satan's helpers are on to you and they are being told you are helping me." Allah said pay them no mind they are too involved with changing the Bible in all these churches especially Notre Dame." Notre Dame will burn one day for all this evil taking place in it. How will it start said Michel? Allah said angels will start the fire after God sends them when he finds out his name was taken from the Bible in this church by these helpers of Satan. They will try and rebuild it and God will burn it again. Allah told Michel I want you to start a secret society called the free masons. Allah told Michel I will tell you what to tell them, it will be important in the end times. The Apostle Paul or Michel did as Allah had asked and formed a secret society known as the free masons. Michel asked Allah, why are they called Free Masons? It is because they are free of the Catholic Church's control. Kings and Queens along with many hierarchy people belong to this society. We will tell them how to prepare for the end times. Allah said I want you to get word to the Knights Templar and get them ready to disappear when they will be hunted down and killed. Allah told Michel the plan and he carried out Allah's plan. They must all go into hiding said Michel to the Knights Templar after they plant the Dead Sea scrolls in Jerusalem.

CHAPTER 24

Satan meets with Hitler (Hisler) and they talk about their plan to take over the world and Hitler's plan to kill all the Jews so he can change the Old-Testament. So Satan tells Hitler to start killing the Jews. So Hitler started rounded up all the Jewish people and then Hitler had his soldiers executing them and then burying their bodies but this took too much time and was too expensive. So Hitler had them all brought to be gassed and then burned in the oven's. This went on for some time until the war was over and Hitler was defeated. Hitler wanted to destroy the world and take it over, he was hoping to satisfy Satan and get his plan going with taking over the world. Hitler ended up killing himself rather than getting caught by the allied army. Satan then found out his plan was not working out and wanted to destroy the Jews from other directions. He then tried to kill them with the by wars after they formed the country of Israel. Allah was working with Noel on how to get the world together under Gods plan so the people would have no more religious wars and work together. Allah told Noel that he was tired but his hatred for Satan was solid. Noel said father you must remain strong so Satan cannot destroy the people, Allah said Noel I will be strong like you were when Satan tested you.

CHAPTER 25

Satan started this Corona virus by tempting the people as he always does. Knowing full well the implications this would have upon the world. I have spoken with God about the knowledge of these diseases and how susceptible the population is and how easy, it spreads. If Satan gets his hands on the right disease he could kill everyone on this planet in 5 months. God put extra angels on security of the vault in heaven before returning to creating the universe. Allah God said you and Noel watch over the people why I work on the universe. Now I want you to look up the word janitor it means keeper of the door or keeper of the gate. This is important I am a janitor and God picked me and told me to become a janitor and this has significance because God is telling you to look for the one who opens doors it is in the Bible, God wants you to find the janitor. The janitor has the keys to open the door to heaven.

CHAPTER 26

Oceanna was carrying her baby Noel down to the lake to gather water for the evening meal. Oceanna was walking through the trees and met Satan and his creation Hisler on her way to the lake. Satan said Oceanna where is Allah at you should not wonder through the woods all alone. Oceanna kept walking and Hisler stepped in front of Oceanna and said let me see your baby. Baby Noel began to cry and Oceanna said please leave me alone, and went around Hisler. Satan said please show us your baby Oceanna. Then another angel Gabriel was walking up from the trail and heard the baby crying and said hi Oceanna are you alright miss. Satan said we just want to see the baby we mean no harm. Oceanna said to Gabriel thankyou I am just trying to gather water for our meal I am in a hurry, I have food cooking. Satan smiled and said perhaps another time when you are not in a hurry Oceanna. Oceanna never said anything to Allah because she knew Allah and Satan were friends.

CHAPTER 27

Noel was almost equivalent to 13 years old in Earth years. The angels sent Noel to the market in heaven to purchase items for the evening meal he would have with angels he was staying with while Allah was watching over Gods creation with Oceanna. Noel was purchasing items for the salad and met Satan and his creation Hisler. Hisler said to Noel when you were a baby we asked your Mother Oceanna to show us what you looked like. Noel said to Hisler you are a hideous man who created you, it couldn't have been God? Satan got angry and said Hisler is my friend, I created Hisler. Hisler said why are you not living with your Mother and Father? Noel said my parents are watching over Gods creation on Earth, you know that Satan and you should know that to Hisler. I heard you tried to trick some of the people to eat from the tree of knowledge. Hisler smiled along with Satan and Satan said we will be dealing with you soon enough, we will see what Allah does when I tempt you, yes we will I can wait tell that time comes! Noel said you can tempt me all you want Satan, I will never betray my Mother or Father.

CHAPTER 28

Then I remember God talking to Abraham it was a rainy day, it had not rained for months prior to this day but today it rained a little bit. Abraham took Isaac with him as we went out to the rock with a couple sheep. Abraham was silent and Isaac just followed his father out in the desert, then we came to the small hill and climbed it to the rock. God wanted to see if Abraham would sacrifice his son Isaac as he told him he wanted him to. Abraham looked all around the rock, and God said right here Abraham is where I want you. Abraham placed Isaac on the rock and kissed him and raised the knife and God said stop Abraham. Abraham stopped and God said Abraham I will bless all your descendants and they will become nations for all time. God then told Abraham to sacrifice one of the sheep and he did, I remember exactly where on the rock Abraham placed Isaac and then I woke up.

CHAPTER 29

Then I remember when Muhammad died and we walked to the rock, I said follow me Muhammad and we got to the rock it was deadly silent that night and I told Muhammad to first climb on the small rock and then step on the main rock. This was on the other side of the rock where Abraham placed Isaac. God said remember where Muhammad is stepping it will be important one day and looked at the rock and I remembered. Muhammad said Allah are you taking me to heaven, I said yes Muhammad. It was a long walk to get to the rock and I needed to talk to God, Satan was going to change another book the book the Quran. I was angry and sad for Muhammad's people because they would be deceived by Satan. Then again I woke up.

CHAPTER 30

Noel met with his father Allah and Allah said Noel when you take up flesh as Jesus it is going to take a little while for you to get all your memories being Noel do you understand? Noel said yes, Allah said Noel your Mother and I will be with you until it is time for you to die and become Noel again do you understand. Noel said yes father, I love you father and I love you Noel said Allah. Satan is going to tempt you and try to get me to interfere with it. You must be strong Noel and not give into this temptation. I will not interfere, Satan will not win said Allah. When you have risen from the dead touch no one until you see me, I want all the sins of the world. Yes father said Noel. Allah told Noel this is all part of the plan to get all the people to heaven. Then Noel went with the angels to be born and take up flesh. Allah kissed his son goodbye for now. Allah went down and found Mary and placed the seed of Noel inside of her. When Jesus was tempted by Satan, what Satan changed was what Jesus said. The Bible says Jesus said do not tempt the lord thy God it should say do not tempt my father Allah or my Mother Oceanna, this was changed in the Bible by the two Popes Innocent.

CHAPTER 31

Allah remembers his talk with his son Jesus, Jesus said explain to me Father (Allah) why does Satan want this world destroyed and all the people destroyed. Allah said Satan is not the same angel he was when we were friends he is jealous and this jealousy is so powerful that it has overtaken his mind. It is all he thinks about, is wanting to destroy me and what-ever I love and who-ever I love. Satan's way of serving God is to be my adversary. Why does God allow it father, asked Jesus. Allah said God is fair and does not want to destroy anything until they do not listen and stop worshipping him, he gives you many, many chances to learn from your mistakes. But Satan is pure hatred and evil now father said Jesus. Allah said yes I know but God still feels he can change. When we teach people to worship God we are saving them, don't people understand if they stop worshipping God, God is going to destroy them Father (Allah). No said Allah they do not understand that, that is why it is so important that we teach them that. Jesus said when they change the Bible and take you and Mother out of the Bible and make me God don't they understand God is going to destroy them? Allah said Jesus they do not understand that, even my own Mother when I take up flesh will refuse the truth, it is all they know, and the way they were taught. But Father God is going to send them right back down here again if he does not destroy them. I know said Allah, Jesus we must keep trying to teach them so Satan does not win and destroy them.

CHAPTER 32

Allah remembers his conversation with his bride Oceanna. Oceanna you are teaching them very well except for killing one another. Oceanna said Allah some things are left for you to teach as they looked at the Inca's. I think it is just in their nature to be destructive after the fruit from the tree of knowledge. Allah why do you have to take up flesh and be with that woman (Paula) she is going to hate you in the end. I need a son to run things on Earth when I come back to you and retire. How else can these things be achieved, I cannot send Noel, you can only take up flesh once as an angel, you know Gods Law Oceanna. Oceanna said yes but I really hate this woman. Now Oceanna it will be fine, I love you more than anything you know that and after we will be together for ever. Oceanna said kiss me Allah. Allah took Oceanna in his arms and kissed her with a kiss that lasted forever as he smelled her lovely hair and touched her tongue with his own and kissed her neck and then said to watch over him while he takes up flesh and battles Satan. Oceanna started crying as Allah walked away.

CHAPTER 33

Jeff (Allah) suddenly remembered feeling mentally ill. Allah was experiencing psychotropic events in his mind where he heard Satan laughing but he knew Satan was not there but it felt real. Allah knew he needed help with this as Allah suddenly felt the full force of the schizophrenia and Noel said Father you need to seek help with this through the Veterans Association hospital it is part of the plan God has for you. Allah told his brother to take him to the hospital in Mankato, Minnesota. Allah spent several days at a county crises help facility. Allah had a burning on his neck where Satan tried to mark him but it did not work. Allah then went home but rechecked himself back in to the crisis center. Allah started medication for schizophrenia but it was not a strong enough dose and it was not handling the voices and things Allah seen, he seen people suffering from a disease which he would later discover was the Corona Virus and he could not deal with the laughing from Satan. Allah went back to the Mankato hospital and said that he was fighting Satan and needed help with the voices and his medication was not working. So the Mankato doctor had Jeff taken to the VA. In Minneapolis. Here Jeff was prescribed a stronger medication. Jeff thought Satan sent Osama bin Laden after him as another person looked like him. The nurses told Jeff know that is not Osama Bin Laden. Allah made a full recovery he thought and checked back out of the hospital. Jeff spent a short time at home and then the schizophrenia crept back into his life. Again Satan tried to brand him on his neck. Allah went out to the garage and looked at his dog Smokey and heard Satan laughing and thought it came from his dog Smokey, Jeff went in and got his k-bar and pulled the knife from the sheath and was going to kill Smokey and then he heard Noel yell no Father that is not Satan. Jeff put Smokey outside in the fenced in back yard with some food and water and got into his Bronco II and went to Butternut Lutheran Church and turned off the truck and begin praying to God and Asked for Noel's help. He heard Satan on the radio station, Satan was telling Jeff to kill himself. Jeff than started his Bronco II and left for his Mothers and Step-Fathers farm house at LaSalle and he went inside quietly and laid down on the couch. Jeff laid there and then dawn broke and heard the pet turkey outside squawking and got off the couch in anger and went out and seen the turkey and thought he seen Satan inside the turkey and grabbed it and suffocated the turkey. Then heard God say that is not Satan Allah. Then Jeff went inside the house and pulled out a large butcher knife and went to two rocks and placed the knife over his finger damaged by Satan and thought he could cut off Satan by cutting off the finger. Jeff picked up the other rock and raised it while holding the knife over the finger and slammed the rock down on the knife. The knife cut the finger deep but only broke the bone in the finger. Jeff went back inside the house and the finger was bleeding badly by then. Jeff grabbed a towel and woke up his Mother and explained what happened and Bev said were taking you back to the Minneapolis VA. So his step-father took the turkey to the back of the house and then they all piled into the car for the Minneapolis VA. Jeff got there and just kept saying my son is going to help me, Jesus is going to help me. The doctor stitched my finger shut and then I went to my assigned room and I told Satan one day I will kill you. Allah got prescribed the right medicine for schizophrenia and made a full recovery a few weeks later.

CHAPTER 34

Allah meets with God on the end of the Universe. God says Allah how is my plan proceeding? Allah says God, Satan has unleashed a virus on the world of Earth. God says tell me more about it. Allah explains to God all the circumstances and waits for God to reply. Allah says God, Satan is getting out of hand and? God stops Allah and says you want to kill him. Allah says you know how I feel about Satan I cannot hide it from you God. God says you love all the people that is why I chose you over Satan to create man women and child. Without love Allah it is just dust. Allah said God I will always do what- ever you ask but Satan is making that difficult for me to accomplish. God said if it was easy I would have picked someone else but I picked you Allah. I will speak to Satan said God, now continue with the plan. Yes God said Allah.

CHAPTER 35

Allah was in his home and smelled Satan, it smelled like sewage. Allah said what do you want now Satan, to try and kill me before I complete the plan? Satan wields absolute power over you when you are his apprentice and rapes you with psychological manipulations beyond anything I could write in this book or even words can describe. Homosexual rape is just one area of power he garners over you. Why do you think the mind of his apprentice is the way it is, Satan destroys the mind. Some are attracted to this tell they find out what it is, why do you think there were so many priests attracted to the Catholic religion who were homosexual, Satan was calling them to it. You do not want Satan having this kind of power over you but for some it is too late unless they change their ways. The only one who has power in that situation is Satan and you just do what he tells you to do. You become a demon which is a zombie controlled by Satan, everything that you once were is gone. Satan takes your mind and well-being and all that you are this is your soul. But do not worry Noel my son and I Allah will never let that happen and Satan will never win. Satan said I will destroy you soon enough Allah and left the house.

CHAPTER 36

Allah thought on Gods plan and talked with Noel and Oceanna in secret with God. Allah said Noel Satan is going to keep hatching these viruses now that he has knowledge of how to do it. Noel said yes father it is all tied to destroying all of this world. Allah said Noel you have to guard the vault in heaven with your most trusted angels and they talked about who could handle the job. Satan wants to cut a deal and get his apprentices back in the book of life and I just cannot allow Hitler, Napoleon, or Osama Bin Laden to terrorize the people and kill innocent human beings. We have to be very watchful for Satan and his demons. Oceanna I know you would like to kill him with a tornado, volcano, or earthquake but he just will not take up flesh and fight me said Allah. If I cut a deal and allow his apprentices back in the book of life if they all face me on the battlefield at Armagetto. Yes father do you think he will take the deal said Noel? He is a coward but it is his only chance to get his demons life.

CHAPTER 37

Allah remembers what happened after his son Noel was crucified on the cross. Oceanna was so angry she headed for Rome, the vast majority of Romans were celebrating near a place called Pompeii. Oceanna's anger was enormous as she blew a volcano right down on the Romans with ash killing the vast majority of Romans. Oceanna turned the skies dark, because the darkness came from the ash from the volcano in the sky after Jesus was crucified and blew over Israel. Paul the Apostle went to Rome after many years and Peter convinced what was left of Romans to turn to Christianity or they would be destroyed. Peter started his church in Rome but Jesus warned Peter Satan would use him as it still is in the Bible though how Peter was used was taken out by Satan's two Popes Innocent. Because they were the ones using Peter to do Satan's bidding. Oceanna was never the same after her son's murder and spent her time working with the Inca Indians. Allah continued to work with the remaining Apostles especially Paul. Paul asked Allah, "What will become of me when I die Allah?" Paul said Allah will I go to heaven even after all those people I murdered when I was Saul? Allah said Paul I will take you to heaven but I will have to convince God to judge you by your next life. Paul said Allah who will I be in the next life? Allah said a very gifted person who can predict the future. Paul said Allah I cannot predict the future how am I going to do that? Allah said I am going to tell you the future you just have to write it down Paul. Paul said that does not sound so tough what is my name Allah? Allah said Michael Nostradamus will be your new name Paul. Jesus said on the cross, "Forgive them Mother for they know not what they do." Satan had his Two Popes Innocent change it too, "Forgive them father for they know not what they do taking Oceanna's story and character out of the Bible. The two Popes Innocent had worshippers pray to Jesus human Mother rather than Jesus angel Mother because they hated Oceanna for what she did to the Romans at Pompeii. Anyone caught praying to Mother Earth was considered a witch or praying to Oceanna that is where it all started.

CHAPTER 38

Allah thought to himself how much this world has cost him and his family but how many people they have seen touched by Gods word and how their life has changed theirs. Where would he have been back in heaven with his son and bride with only them to think about and nothing else how small and empty his world would be without the many, many friends he has made along the way and how much he has been inspired by the new vision God had that he developed in man and women and child after them. The impossibilities of not knowing how to handle defeat and triumph is all part of the joy in discovering love and how far it will go and indeed it has gone far, Satan will never know these joys only God and my family enjoy for his hate and jealousy clouds all that has happened for these ones called man and women as they learn to live and love. Allah remembers his son Noel and wanted to explain why Jesus called God his Father. In heaven and with the language shared between God and his angels. God is referred to as Jesus father or grandfather but grandfather does not appear in the language which is why God is referred to as just Father. Where Allah is called Jesus birth father, this appears in the language which means Allah is the father to meet the requirement of birth. I hope this clears up any misconceptions drawn from not understanding the language differences.

CHAPTER 39

It was a dark time in the church the two Popes Innocent had just changed the stories about Jesus, and taken Jesus Father Allah and Mother Oceanna out of the Bible and replaced Allah with God and Holy Spirit. Anna and Elsa played at the back of the church as the people started to leave the Catholic Church Notre Dame de Paris. Those stories are not true they whispered to one another, what are we going to do our men are in Jerusalem fighting the war. Elsa asked her Mother what is wrong mommy? Nothing said Elsa's Mother and they left the church. Let us meet tonight and discuss it. All people were very religious and knew every story by heart as it was told to them by the priest and the two Popes Innocent were not having an easy time convincing the people of the new stories and how the church wanted them told. Only the priest was allowed to read from the Bible and the Two Popes Innocent thought this would be easy changing God's word and implementing Satan's plan. The people met in small groups all over Paris and discussed what to do about these untrue stories. So they said they would speak to the priest and send letters to the Pope Innocent. Pope Innocent got word of this and asked Satan what do I do, the people say the stories being told are untrue? Satan looked at the Pope and said kill all of them who do not except our stories. Witch trials began for women who were said to be trying to read the Bible on their own. They were found guilty and either hanged or burned at the stake. Since orphanages were unheard of at this time they killed the children with the Mother if there was no one to take them. King James of England came back from the Holy wars in Jerusalem and was confronted with this problem and had a Bible made in English for him and he wanted people to be able to read it themselves. This changed everything in the world. Pope Innocent had one question for Satan, what are we going to tell the men when they return from the war in Jerusalem and see that we killed all their women and children? Satan smiled and said tell them they died of the Plague.

The End

Printed in the United States
By Bookmasters